"IT'S A BIT SMALL, ISN'T IT?"

I turned round. There, standing on the display table, was a man. A great big bearded man, in a sort of Ancient Greek tunic, with a temple on his head.

My temple.

Or rather, bits of my temple. He'd got the roof on, all right, and the cardboard pillars were dangling from it round his forehead. Which looked a bit daft, actually, since they were made from loo rolls . . .

ZEUS on the LOOSE!

John Dougherty

illustrated by Georgien Overwater

YOUNG CORGI BOOKS

A YOUNG CORGI BOOK 9780552550819

Published in Great Britain by Young Corgi Books,
An imprint of Random House Children's Books

This edition published 2004

7 9 10 8 6

The Random House Group Limited supports The Forest Stewardship
Council (FSC), the leading international forest certification organisation.
All our titles that are printed on Greenpeace approved FSC certified paper
carry the FSC logo. Our paper procurement policy can be found at:
www.randomhouse.co.uk/environment.

Mixed Sources
Product group from well-managed
forests and other controlled sources
www.fsc.org Cert no. TT-COC-2139
© 1996 Forest Stewardship Council

Set in Bembo MT Schoolbook

Young Corgi Books are published by Random House Children's Books,
61–63 Uxbridge Road, London W5 5SA,
A Random House Group Company

Addresses for companies within The Random House Group Limited
can be found at: www.randomhouse.co.uk/offices.htm

THE RANDOM HOUSE GROUP Limited Reg. No. 954009
www.**kids**at**randomhouse**.co.uk

A CIP catalogue record for this book is available from the British Library.

Printed and bound in Great Britain by
CPI Cox & Wyman, Reading, RG1 8EX

Chapter One

Temples

This is me.

And this is the Greek god Zeus. You say it like 'Zyoos'.

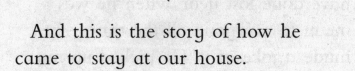

And this is the story of how he came to stay at our house.

It all started at school. We'd been learning about Ancient Greece, and now we were doing a project about Greek gods. In this particular lesson we were making model temples.

I was doing a temple of Zeus. Really good, it was. Looked just like the genuine article. Except smaller, of course. And the real temple probably didn't have FREE INSIDE! GREAT SPECIAL OFFER! all over the roof, because it probably wouldn't have been made out of a cornflakes box.

But other than that, it was really good. Everyone said so.

Even Troy. Troy used to be horrible, but he's been trying ever so hard to be good this term. So instead of telling me it was rubbish – like he'd have done last year, when he was mean to everyone all the time – he made a joke of it. He picked up my

2

temple and started speaking into it in
a big deep funny voice:

"Hey, Zeus! Are you in there? Come
and look at this really great temple
that Alex made for you!"

Everyone laughed – even Miss Wise.
I wouldn't have laughed if I'd
known what was going to happen.

After school I stayed behind. My mum works in the school most days, hearing children in the infant classes read, and I usually stay till she's ready to come home.

So I was tidying up for Miss Wise, who was in a staff meeting, when suddenly, behind me, there was this big booming voice. You know when you go to the cinema, and they have the trailers, and a man with a very sore throat tells you about the film they're showing soon with exploding helicopters and someone saving the world? It was like that, but even more boomy and echoey. And what it said was:

"IT'S A BIT SMALL, ISN'T IT?"

Boy, did I jump. When you're in school, the scariest voice you expect to hear is the headteacher's — but she can't do a voice anything like this one.

I turned round. There, standing on the display table, was a man. A great big bearded man, in a sort of Ancient Greek tunic, with a temple on his head.

My temple.

Or rather, bits of my temple. He'd got the roof on, all right, and the cardboard pillars were dangling from it round his forehead. Which looked a bit daft, actually, since they were made from loo rolls.

The rest of the temple, he was standing on. All my little plasticine

priests and sacrifices and stuff –
ruined. I'd have been furious if I
hadn't been so scared.

The big man stepped down off the
table.

"NOT VERY STRONG, EITHER,"
he boomed. Lightning danced around
his forehead as he spoke, and the
windows rattled. "WOULDN'T
STAND UP IN A LIGHT SHOWER,
NEVER MIND IF I SMOTE IT
WITH A THUNDERBOLT!"

The whole room seemed to shake,
and a mug wobbled off Miss Wise's
desk and smashed on the floor.
Broken pottery and cold coffee went
everywhere. Mostly on the big man.

"DID I DO THAT?" he boomed.
Then he looked down at his bare,
wet feet.

"Oh, *yuk*!" he said to himself in a
suddenly much more normal tone.

"Me and my big shouty voice! Just *look* at this tunic! I'll *never* get this stain off!"

Well, I was still scared, but not quite *so* scared. It's difficult to be terrified of someone who's worried about getting

7

a coffee stain off a tunic which – to be honest – looks a bit like a girl's dress. So I spoke up.

"Um – excuse me," I said. The big man looked up, one hand dabbing at the stain.

"What is it?" he said – and then seemed to remember himself, and said, "YES, O MORTAL?"

yes, O MORTAL

The room vibrated again, and a second cup leaped off the desk and smashed on the floor. Cold coffee splashed up again, soaking the man's bottom.

"Oh, *poo!*" he said crossly. "*Now*

8

look. It's absolutely *ruined*."

"Um . . ." I said again.

"Yes, yes, go on, I'm listening," the man said, turning round to try and see the stain on his bottom.

"Well . . . who are you, and why are you wearing my temple on your head?" The man started to laugh – a huge great laugh that rattled the windows all over again. He suddenly stopped and clamped his hand over his mouth, looking warily at Miss Wise's desk which still had three or four mugs, half-full of cold coffee, on it.

She's a bit like that, Miss Wise is. Clearing those up was going to be my next job.

Once he was sure the other mugs were staying where they were, the man looked at me again.

"*Your* temple, did you say?" I nodded. He laughed again, but this

I ♥ coffee.

time without the booming. "And you're the god of what, exactly? Cold drinks? Tidying up? Sorry, kid, but I can't see *anyone* worshipping you, never mind building a temple to do it in. No, this is definitely *my* temple," he went on, taking it off his head and waving it in my face. "Not that it's

much of a temple – being all tiny and falling apart like that the moment a decent-sized god appears in it – but you can't be too choosy these days."

I narrowed my eyes. "What do you mean, it's yours? *I* built it," I said.

"Oh, you did, did you?" he said. "And what is it, then?"

"It's the Temple of Zeus," I answered. *And it was the best one in the class until you came along and put it on your head,* I nearly added.

"Aha! Got you!" he grinned. "It's the Temple of Zeus – and *I'm* Zeus, so it's *my* temple, whoever built it, and nur-nur-nee-nur-nur to you, Alex, kiddo." He paused, looking at the temple again, before adding, "By the way – what's the great special offer inside?"

Well, of course, I didn't believe for a moment he was Zeus, but . . . wait

a minute . . .

"How do you know my name?" I demanded.

He rolled his eyes.

"It was in the prayer, stupid."

"What prayer? I don't remember hearing a prayer."

Zeus – if that's who he was – sighed. "Well, *I* heard it," he said, "and that's what counts. Someone prayed in my temple. Like this." Suddenly his voice changed. It was Troy's voice – or rather, the silly

13

voice Troy had put on — that came out of his mouth, saying, *"Hey, Zeus! Are you in there? Come and look at this really great temple that Alex made for you!"*

Then he spoke in his own voice again. "So I came to see. And I've got to say, Alex — this is probably the worst temple I've ever, but *ever* appeared in."

the best!

the worst

I was beginning to get pretty fed up.

"Well, in that case, why don't you just buzz off? Anyway, that wasn't a prayer, it was just messing around."

Zeus shrugged his shoulders. "He was in my temple – or at least his voice was – and he was speaking to me. I count that as a prayer. When you get as few prayers as I do these days, you can't afford to be choosy. So, *that* was a prayer, *this* is a temple, and since there's nobody else here, I hereby appoint *you* as my High Priest. Come on, let's go back to your house."

Well, as you can imagine, I wasn't having that.

"No way!" I said. "There is absolutely *no way*, Zeus! No flipping WAY!!! What'll my mum say if I come home with a whacking great Greek god in a coffee-stained dress?"

He smiled.

15

"Don't worry," he said. "She won't even know I'm there. Or at least — she won't even know it's me. Us Greek gods can do the most *amazing* things."

Which is how I came home that day with a talking hamster called Zeus. And how a top-of-the-range luxury hamster-cage just magically appeared in my room. And why I had to spend the evening making another temple for school.

Two more, in fact.

Zeus chewed up the first one and made a nest.

Chapter Two

Sacrifices

I woke up the next morning earlier than usual. Quite a bit earlier, in fact. Three whole *hours* earlier. The reason being, Zeus – back in his own shape again – was bouncing up and down on the end of my bed shouting, "WAKE UP, YOU LAZY HIGH PRIEST! TIME FOR MY MORNING SACRIFICE!"

I sat bolt upright.

"Shut *up*, you idiot!" I hissed. "You'll have Mum and Dad in here in a moment!"

Zeus stopped bouncing. His face got very cross all of a sudden, and little bolts of lightning started dancing around his head.

"Idiot?" he complained. "*Idiot?!?* I am the great and mighty Zeus, mortal, and you've got ten seconds to give me one good reason I shouldn't smite you here and now!"

There was a terrible flickering in his right hand, as if an entire thunderstorm was curled up in there.

"Well," I answered as

calmly as I could – though to be honest I was pretty cross myself, not having had enough sleep – "if you smite me, who's going to be your High Priest?"

Zeus hopped down off the bed.

"Fair point," he admitted. "Why don't you just say sorry and I'll forgive you? I'd hate to have to do the sacrifice myself – kind of takes the fun out of it."

If I hadn't been so tired, I might have argued, but it seemed easier just to apologize.

"Sorry," I said, closing my eyes. "Can I go back to sleep now?"

"No way!" Zeus said. "I told you – it's time for my morning sacrifice, and since you're the High Priest, you've got to do it. Unless you'd like me to smite you, of course."

I sat up.

"OK," I grumbled. "What do I have to . . . ?" And then I noticed what he was wearing. I groaned.

"Zeus," I said, "what *have* you got on?"

"Do you like it?" he grinned. "I found it in a cupboard outside your room. It's an even nicer tunic than mine, isn't it?"

"No," I told him. "It's not. It isn't a tunic at all. You're wearing my mum's best nightie."

"It looks like a tunic," he said huffily.

"It's not a tunic," I told him again. "It's a nightie. Ladies wear them. Men don't."

"Well, I've got to wear *something*," he sulked. "And I can't wear my own tunic. It's ruined. You're the High Priest – *do* something. Come on, I *command* you to do something! Get me a tunic! I want a tunic!"

"OK, OK," I told him. "I'll get you a tunic in a minute. One thing at a time, though. Tell me about this sacrifice. What do I have to do?"

"Oh, yes," he said, clapping his hands together, all smiles again. "Well, what my priests used to do, back in the old days, was get the best bull they could find, take it to the temple, kill it in my honour, and then roast it on the fire."

"Why?" I asked.

"I like the smell of roast bull."

"And?"

ahem

"Nothing else. Roast bull just smells nice. It's a great way to start the day, with the smell of roast bull in your nostrils."

"What happened then?" I asked.
"Didn't you come down from Mount
Olympus on a cloud and eat the bull
they'd cooked for you?"

Zeus looked disgusted.

"Yuk! No *way!*" he said. "roast bull
smells great, but I can't *stand* the taste
of mortal food. Give me nectar and
ambrosia any day!"

"Well," I told him, "roast bull is out.
But if it's just the smell you like, I can
probably manage something. Fair
enough?"

Zeus sighed. "My fault for choosing
an eight-year-old High Priest,
I suppose. OK – but it's *got* to be
in a temple. I absolutely *insist*
on that."

I reminded him that the only temple
we had handy was the one I'd made
the evening before, but he was
determined. A sacrifice wasn't really a

sacrifice unless it was done under the temple roof, he said.

Which is how, a few minutes later, I found myself down in the kitchen, wearing a cardboard temple on my head and sacrificing a toasted bacon sandwich to a Greek god who was dressed in an old bed-sheet.

"Don't forget the prayers," Zeus said.

"I don't know any prayers," I said, "not Ancient Greek ones, anyway."

"Don't worry," he said, "you can just tell me how great I am and ask me for help with your day, that kind of thing."

So there I was, buttering the toast, waiting for yesterday's leftover bacon to finish warming in the microwave, and muttering stuff like:

"Oh, Zeus, you're really great at turning into a hamster . . . and, er,

that trick with the booming voice is
really terrific . . . and your tunic is
ever so white and clean – the one

you're wearing now, I mean,
obviously, not the one with coffee-
stains all over it . . . anyway, please
help me to have a good day by – by
not getting me into trouble or
anything, and not doing the booming
voice near Miss Wise's desk when she's
got mugs of cold coffee on it . . ."

Meanwhile Zeus was sitting there
sniffing the bacon and toast and
saying, "Well, it's not as nice as roast
bull but I suppose it'll do . . ."

Then the kitchen door opened and in walked my dad.

"Alex," he groaned, "do you know what time it is? What on earth are you doing?"

Well, it was no use trying to pretend, was it? So I told him.

"I'm making a sacrifice to Zeus, Dad."

He blinked.

"Let me get this straight, son. You're down in the kitchen at half-past five in the morning, wearing your homework on your head and sacrificing a bacon sandwich to a hamster?"

I looked round. There was Zeus, back in hamster-shape, sitting on the kitchen table looking all innocent and

cleaning his fur.

"Well, um, yeah . . . Charlie says he likes it . . ." Charlie was the friend I'd pretended to borrow the hamster from. I made a mental note to tell him I'd borrowed his hamster called Zeus who liked sacrifices of bacon sandwiches – just in case Mum or Dad bumped into him.

"Alex," Dad said, "what have your mother and I said about using the microwave?

Not to mention the toaster?"

I blushed and looked at my slippers. "*Don't use them unless you're with me, Dad,*" I mumbled.

"Too right!" Dad said. "Not very safe, is it?"

I shook my head.

Dad hadn't finished. "Do you know," he demanded, "what is the only thing – the *only* thing, mind you – stopping me from smacking your behind and sending you back to bed?"

I shook my head again.

"It's this: that sandwich smells great! Go on, pour on the ketchup and share it out!"

That's my dad for you. I think he taught me to use the microwave so there'd be more food for him.

"Can't have the hamster on the table, though. Come on, little fella, into your cage." He reached out and lifted Zeus up. "Ow! That's weird! Felt like a little electric shock there! You been rubbing this hamster on a balloon, Alex?" And he carried Zeus upstairs and back to the cage – not noticing the angry little flashes of lightning round the hamster's head.

Chapter Three

The War of Troy

As you can imagine, I was pretty tired by the time I got to school. I'd tried to get back to sleep after Dad and I finished eating the sacrifice, but Zeus was sulking in the hamster-cage – and sulking pretty loudly, for a hamster.

"No way to treat the King of the Gods, that's for sure," he kept saying in a little hamsterish voice. "Anyway, nobody except the priest is meant to eat the sacrifice. Blasphemy, that's what it is. Ought to smite him. Well – *tried* to smite him. Not my fault if hamsters can't smite properly . . ."

And so on. And so on. So that I

31

didn't get a wink of sleep between then and school-time.

I had to get to school early that morning. I had to put my new temple where the old one had been, before Miss Wise got in. Zeus was still grumbling when we got to the classroom.

"I'll show him . . . next time, I'll be a guinea pig!" he was saying as I swapped the temples, stuffing the old battered one into my pocket. "Bet guinea pigs are better at smiting . . .

No, not guinea pigs – electric eels. I always get those two mixed up. Oooh, yeah, I'll be an electric eel, a really big one, and then when he picks me up I'll smite him good and proper! He'll think twice before putting *me* in a cage halfway through a sacrifice . . ."

And so on. And so on.

It got worse when lining-up time came.

You see, we'd decided that I couldn't keep a hamster hidden all day, so he turned himself into some kind of bug. I didn't ask what sort. I didn't even look when he did it because then he hid himself in my ear. I was really worried someone else would see and go, "*Eeeeurgh!* Alex has a bug in his ear!"

What really *really* worried me was that Hélène would see and go, "*Eeeeurgh!* Alex has a bug in his ear!"

Hélène only came to our school about a week ago. She's from France. Miss Wise put her next to me on the carpet because I knew the French for "Hello, how are you?"

Actually, Hélène probably doesn't know the English for 'bug', but it would be *so* embarrassing if she saw Zeus and thought that I'd got nits.

Anyway, we went into school, and sat on the carpet. And all the time, Zeus was still going on and on and on. It was maddening, especially as I couldn't say anything, because:

1) Miss Wise would think I was talking to one of the other kids and tell me off, and what could I say? I could hardly tell her, "Sorry, miss, I have a Greek god in my ear disguised as a beetle and he won't stop going on and on about smiting my dad for putting him in a cage and eating his bacon sandwich."

2) Hélène might think I was nuts, muttering to myself, and then she might make a fuss about sitting next to me, and that would be really embarrassing.

Then, after the register, Miss Wise started reading from *The Book of Greek Myths and Legends*, and that got really difficult because Zeus started making comments.

The first bit she read went like this: "'It is my will and my desire,' said the mighty Zeus, High King of the Gods

on Olympus, 'to cause the glorious war of Troy, which shall be remembered for all time.'"

"Oooh," Zeus whispered in my ear, "I didn't say it half so well as that! All I remember saying was, 'It's been a while since we saw a good punch-up. Let's get the Greeks started on the Trojans.'"

Miss Wise went on: "Zeus called for Ares, the god of war, and ordered him to ready himself for the conflict, which should be the greatest ever known. 'It is my duty and my pleasure to obey, O Most High,' Ares replied."

"He never!" Zeus said. "He's a right moaning minnie, that Ares. What he *actually* said was, 'Oh, do I *have* to? I was looking forward to having a nice rest at the seaside this year! All that

screaming and shouting humans do when they're killing each other gives me a right headache sometimes!' He went *on* and *on* and *on* . . ."

It was a good story. What happened was that this Greek prince married the most beautiful woman in the world. She was called Helen. But Paris, the prince of Troy, fell in love with Helen and took her back to Troy with him. Then all the Greek princes

ganged up together and went and had a war with Paris and the Trojans (they were the people who lived in Troy). They fought for ten years but the Greeks couldn't get into Troy because it had this big high wall all round it. So then the Greeks played a trick on the Trojans.

One morning, the Trojans woke up and saw that all the Greek soldiers had gone, and so had their ships, but they'd left a huge wooden horse. So they sent out a few soldiers to investigate. The soldiers came back and said the Greeks had definitely sailed away but they'd built this horse as a present for Poseidon, the

god of the sea, so he'd get them home safely. I don't know why a sea-god wants a big wooden horse, but anyway: the Trojans thought if they took the horse inside their city, Poseidon would bring them good luck, so that's what they did.

But some Greek soldiers were hiding inside the horse, and when it was night and the Trojans were asleep they came out and opened the city gates. Then all the other Greeks, who'd sneaked back, came in and they killed the Trojans and won the war.

Miss Wise read the story really well, and then we did some work about describing words. I thought of a few words to describe Zeus – who was still going on and on and on – but Miss Wise would have kept me in at playtime if I'd used them.

I wish she had. It was at playtime that the trouble really started.

I had to tell Charlie about telling my parents he'd lent me the hamster – in case they saw him and said anything about it. And then I had to tell him about Zeus. And of course he didn't believe me, so I had to ask Zeus to come out of my ear – which gave me a break from all the muttering, anyway – and turn back into a hamster.

Charlie was so amazed he couldn't say a word. And then the hamster sat up straight, and said, "It is my will and my desire to cause the glorious war of Troy, which shall be remembered for all time. Or at least till playtime tomorrow."

I didn't like that last bit.

"What do you mean?" I asked.

"Well," Zeus said, "it's been ages since I saw a decent fight. And I can't really start one like the last war of Troy without Ares to give me a hand, but I reckon we can get a bit of a scrap going over that pretty  little girl you were sitting next to. What's her name?"

I didn't really want to get into this, but Charlie – still gobsmacked – said, "Hélène. She's French."

Zeus was really pleased at this.

"Hélène! Perfect!" he said, clapping his little paws together. "Or nearly. 'Helen' would be better, but beggars can't be choosers. Now, what about that kid who prayed to me? What's his name?"

That got me really worried.

"Leave Troy out of this," I said. "He'll be in real trouble if he gets into a fight . . ."

"Troy?" Zeus squeaked. "That's not right! Troy's the *city*, not a person! Why isn't he called Paris?"

"No," Charlie said, "Paris is a city.

It's in France."

"You don't know what you're talking about, Nelly No-Brain," Zeus insisted. "I've done this before, and anyway, I'm a god and you're not. Just listen:  Troy is a city, and Paris comes and takes Helen there and then we start a fight. OK?"

"Charlie's right," I said. "Troy's the boy and Paris is the city. That's where Hélène comes from — Paris."

Zeus stamped his little hamster-foot. "No, no, no," he complained, "this is all wrong. Weren't you idiots listening to the story? What's supposed to happen is that Paris takes Helen to Troy. How can he do that if he's a city and Troy isn't? And even if we change it round, Troy can't take Hélène to Paris if that's where she's from in the first place! You lot are spoiling my war and it's not fair!" And with that, he suddenly changed from hamster-shape back into a bearded

man in a bed-sheet.

"I'm fed up with being a hamster," he announced, "and I'm jolly well going to have a war. So there."

And he marched out into the middle of the playground and said in that window-rattling voice:

"HEAR ME, O MORTAL CHILDREN!

45

I AM THE GREAT AND MIGHTY
ZEUS! IT IS MY WILL AND MY
DESIRE TO CAUSE THE
GLORIOUS WAR OF TROY ..."

Chapter Four

Not the War of Troy

I think he was expecting everyone to stand still and listen. But what would you do, if you were having your playtime and this great big loony in a bed-sheet marched out into the playground and started yelling in a voice that made the ground shake?

You'd do what everyone in my school did. You'd run.

And you'd scream.

Suddenly you couldn't hear what Zeus was saying because of the noise of about 300 children all screaming at once and the teacher on duty blowing her whistle like mad to try to get everyone indoors. It was completely crazy.

Charlie and I ran up to Zeus to try and get him away from there.

"LISTEN, O MORTAL CHILDREN!" he was booming. "I SAID, LISTEN! OH, FOR GOODNESS' SAKE, STOP THAT NOISE AND LISTEN! BELT UP!"

"They can't hear you!" I yelled at him. "You're scaring them! Turn back into a hamster, quick!"

"Shan't!" he grumbled. "I'm fed up with being a silly old hamster. Anyway, all I wanted was a decent war. What did they have to go screaming and yelling for?"

"*Please!*" I said. "The teachers will be calling the police to arrest you!"

"Don't care," Zeus replied huffily. "Anyone tries to arrest me, I'll smite them!" Lightning flashed dangerously round his head.

By this time, the screaming children had all raced towards the doors of the school and were trying to get in. The teachers were all busy trying to make sure no one got crushed or trampled in the rush. I reckoned we had a couple of minutes before they noticed that Charlie and I were talking to the nutter in the sheet.

"Charlie!" I said, taking the old battered temple out of my pocket and

49

shoving it on my head. "Quick! Give me your playtime snack!"

Normally, no one stood a chance of getting Charlie's snack away from him, but this time he handed it over without a peep. He was still pretty dazed by the whole thing, I think.

It was a bag of crisps. I looked at the flavour on the packet, and couldn't believe my luck. Quickly, I held the bag under Zeus's nose and opened it.

"Oh, great and mighty Zeus," I gabbled, "in your honour I sacrifice this bag of roast beef – er – roast *bull* flavour crisps and beg you in your wisdom to take us somewhere quiet where we can talk about this!"

Zeus looked down and sniffed. His face brightened and the lightning stopped flashing round his forehead.

"Oh, OK," he said. And suddenly the three of us were standing in the boys' toilets.

"Great smell!" Zeus said. "The crisps, I mean, not the toilets. OK, get on with the prayer."

So I prayed this long prayer about how I begged Zeus not to start a war, and to let us live in peace, and about how war was generally a

Bad Thing, and do you know what he said?

"OK, Alex, nice prayer, great sacrifice, now let's get on with the war."

"Weren't you listening?" I demanded.

"Not really, no. I was smelling the sacrifice. Sometimes I just use the prayer as sort of background music. Anyway, I reckon we could divide the

school into two armies. Big kids against little kids, maybe, or boys against girls . . ."

"Children against teachers?" Charlie suggested. I elbowed him in the ribs and told him to shut up. It was bad enough having a loopy Greek god on my hands without my best friend joining in too.

"Zeus," I said, "listen to me. We are not going to have a war. Even calling

each other rude names is against the rules in this school. If we have a war, Miss Wise will keep the whole class in at playtime for the rest of our lives!"

"Not the ones who get killed," Zeus said.

"Zeus! *No one* is going to get killed. Don't you get it? We're not soldiers, we're kids! Our teachers wouldn't let us have a war even if we wanted one – and we *don't* want one!"

"Oh, boo-hoo, Sally Spoilsport!" Zeus said, rudely. "Where's your sense of history? Don't you want people to sing about your glorious death for years to come?"

"I'd rather have a glorious life for years to come, thanks. Or any kind of life, really. Anyway, we've got to get back to class."

Zeus shook his head.

"Not till we've done the wooden

horse bit," he said. "If we can't have the war, I insist we at least have someone hiding inside a wooden horse."

"We *can't*," I said. "We'll get into trouble!"

"Listen, mortal," he hissed, "either we do the wooden horse bit or I start smiting! So there!" Lightning flashed around his forehead again, and there was a distant rumble.

"Sorry," said Charlie, holding his stomach. "Can I have my crisps back now?"

"They're not yours, they're mine," Zeus snapped. "My High Priest sacrificed them to me, remember? And only the High Priest can eat the sacrifice. Now, where's the wooden horse?"

"All right," I sighed. "Come on, then."

We went to the gym.

"Here it is," I said. "It's called a vaulting horse. We jump over it in PE."

"Vaulting horse?" Zeus said. "*Revolting* horse, more like! It's just a big wooden box with a cushion on it! We can't finish a war we're not actually going to have with the Big Wooden Box With A Cushion On It of Troy! That's just stupid! Come on, get me a proper wooden horse at once, and then let's get it outside the walls."

I was getting really cross now.

"Where do you expect me to get a proper wooden horse from?" I snapped. "I'm not a carpenter!

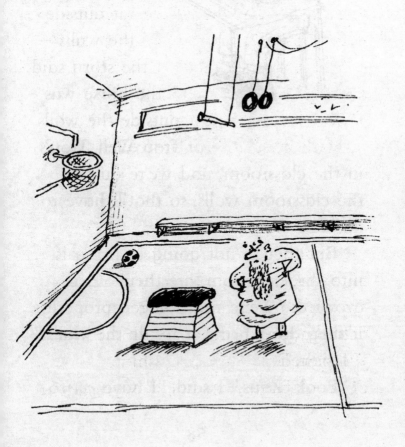

Miss Wise won't even let us use a craft knife until next term, never mind a

saw! This is the best we can do. And as for getting it outside the walls – the story said the horse was outside the walls of Troy. Well, Troy's in the classroom, and we're outside the classroom walls, so that'll have to do."

"But they're not going to bring it into the classroom, are they?" Zeus growled. "We're not doing it properly if they don't bring it inside the walls."

I sighed.

"Look, Zeus," I said, "I have *got* to

get back to class and give Miss Wise an excuse for Charlie being missing before she calls the police."

"Hang on!" Charlie said. "Why can't *I* give her an excuse for *you* not being there?"

"Such as?" I asked.

"Er . . . you're with a Greek god who's making you get inside a wooden horse?"

"*That's* why," I told him. "She's never going to believe that. Just get into the horse and pretend to be a Greek soldier. We'll come and find you in a bit, and you can say you hid here because you were so scared of the loony in the bed-sheet."

I went back to class, feeling a bit worried. I wasn't sure what Miss Wise would say – about me being missing from class and everything. I pushed the door open nervously and everyone turned to look.

And then they all started laughing. I couldn't believe it. What could possibly be so funny? Hélène was giggling, Sam was snorting, Troy was laughing so much he nearly fell off his chair . . .

And then Miss Wise rolled her eyes and said, "Alex! What *are* you doing with that model temple on your head?"

Chapter Five

The Wooden Horse of Troy

I snatched the temple off my head and stuffed it in my pocket. Then I had to stand there for ages feeling embarrassed and waiting for everyone to stop laughing. At least it gave me time to think up an excuse – about Charlie feeling ill and me taking him to the toilets – but I never got to use it, because just as everyone was quietening down and Miss Wise said, "So where have you been, Alex? And where's Charlie? I've just sent a message to the office saying you're not here," Troy shouted out, "Oi, miss! What's the vaulting horse doing outside the school?"

Everyone stood up and stared out of the window. The vaulting horse was there, all right – on the pavement, just outside the main gate. I groaned quietly to myself. If Charlie was in there, he was going to be in real trouble.

I put my hand up.

"Do you want me to go and get Mr Cameron, miss?" I asked.

Miss Wise looked at me suspiciously.

"I think you've been out of my sight quite long enough, Alex," she

said. "I hope you and Charlie haven't got anything to do with this."

I tried to look innocent. She sent one of the girls instead.

Mr Cameron, the schoolkeeper, came into the class a few minutes later to ask for some helpers to bring the horse in.

"I don't think we can take children outside the school gates without permission from their parents," Miss Wise told him. "I'll come and help you get it through the gates and into the playground."

She turned to the class.

"I know it's been a bit of a strange morning," she said, "but can I trust you all to get on with some work quietly while I go and help Mr Cameron?"

"Yes, miss!" Troy and I called out together.

Miss Wise looked at us thoughtfully.

"Perhaps you'd better all come out with me," she said after a moment.

Out in the playground, Mr Cameron and Miss Wise swung open the big black iron gates. The vaulting horse stood innocently outside.

"Best do it in bits," Mr Cameron said. "We'll lift the top bit off first."

I froze. If they did that, they'd be bound to see Charlie. I had no idea what the punishment was for sneaking out of school hidden in a piece of gym apparatus, but I was sure it

would be something horrible. Already they were reaching for the handles to pull the top off the horse. I had to do *something* – but what?

"Hang on, miss!" I yelled. "Why don't you just push it?"

Miss Wise rolled her eyes again. I think she was a bit fed up with me.

"*Because*, Alex," she said, gripping the handles, "the bottom of the horse would get scratched on the tarmac." She looked at Mr Cameron. "Ready?" she said.

"No, it wouldn't, miss!" I said desperately. "It wouldn't get scratched! *It's on a sort of trolley thing with wheels on!* Look!"

I said that last bit as loud as I could. And then I held my breath. Because I knew it wasn't on a trolley – yet. And if Zeus couldn't hear me, or didn't take the hint, I was definitely

going to get the biggest telling-off
ever.

"Don't be ridiculous, Alex!" Miss
Wise said. "I really don't know what's
got into you today, but if it carries
on, you and I are going to have a
serious talk—"

"Hold on, Miss Wise!" Mr Cameron
interrupted. "Take a look at this! He's
right!"

I breathed out again.

Miss Wise and Mr Cameron
scratched their heads a bit and said
things like, "Well, where did
that come from?" and,
"I could've *sworn*
it wasn't there a
moment ago,"
and then
they
shrugged,
and got

behind the horse and began to push.

Then Hélène said, "Miss Wise? What is this thing called?"

"It's called a vaulting horse, Hélène."

Hélène put her hand to her mouth and giggled.

"So this is like the story you were telling us! Of the wooden horse being brought through the big gates!"

And then everyone laughed and started cheering and shouting, "Hooray! The Greeks have given up and gone home!" and things like that.

And as soon as the horse was in the playground, some of us got behind it and helped to push, pretending we were Trojans. Which meant that as I pushed, I could press my ear against the horse and listen. Sure enough, under the noise of everyone laughing, I heard two voices.

"What next?" one of them said.

"Next," said the other, "we wait until they're all asleep and then we let our army in and kill them!"

"Er . . . we haven't got an army, have we?" said the first voice, which of course was Charlie's.

"Good point," the second one – Zeus – said. "We'll just have to jump out and kill them ourselves."

"You're joking!" Charlie said. "There's no *way*! Miss Wise'd be *furious* if I killed her!"

And then there was a bump and my ear got mashed against the horse.

"Come on!" Mr Cameron said. "We can't wheel it up the steps! Time to take the top off!"

And before I could stop them, they did.

There was a moment of shocked silence.

We all stood and stared down at Charlie.

Charlie stared up at us.

And then . . . well, words fail me. He was brilliant. He jumped up and yelled, "Miss Wise! It's you! Oh, thank goodness!"

He scrambled out of the horse and threw his arms around her.

"I thought it was that man!" he gasped. "I thought he was going to catch me!"

Before she knew it, Miss Wise was patting him on the back and saying, "There, there, Charlie! It's all right. You're safe," and Charlie was blurting out this story about how the man in the playground had scared him so much he'd run in and hidden in the vaulting horse. Then he'd felt it

71

being lifted onto the trolley and pushed
out of school, and he'd heard the gates
clang shut, and then he'd heard a police
siren and whoever it was pushing the
horse had run away . . .

Just for a moment, I couldn't believe it.
Charlie isn't exactly the quickest thinker
in the world. How on earth had he come
up with that amazing story?

And then I realized.

I sneaked a look at
his ear. Sure enough, I
could just see this
tiny golden beetle in
there, whispering to
him and telling
him what to say.

The rest of the day
was quite quiet after
that. Some police
officers came and

asked us questions about the man
who had been seen in the
playground, and told us all never to
talk to strangers. Miss Wise
was really nice to
Charlie. Zeus was
happy because he'd
had a sort of Trojan
horse, and was
unbearably pleased
with himself for
having got Charlie
out of trouble. And the
Head held an extra
assembly and told us all there was
obviously a gang of international
gym equipment thieves working in the
area and if ever we saw anyone
suspicious in the playground we
should tell Mr Cameron.

  After school, I popped into the
newsagent to stock up on roast beef

flavoured crisps. As we were leaving, Zeus said to me, "Did you know that after the war of Troy it took Odysseus ten years to get home again?"

I got home as fast as I could, and checked the calendar just in case.

Chapter Six

Gifts for the Gods

In the middle of the night, I was
woken by someone tapping on
the window.

Which is odd, because my bedroom's
on the top floor
of the house.

I got up, went
to the window
and drew back
one of the
curtains. There,
sitting on the
windowsill
outside, was
a magnificent
golden eagle.

75

"About time!" it grumbled. "Come on, you stupid High Priest! Let me in! I've been out here tapping for ages! My beak's getting sore!"

I opened the window and Zeus hopped through. He landed on the carpet and changed himself into a big bearded bloke in a bed-sheet again.

"I was bored," he explained. "So I went out for a flap around. I didn't realize how sore tapping on the window would be. Come on! I need a really special sacrifice to make me feel better!"

"No *way*, Zeus!" I told him, getting back into bed. "It's the middle of the night! Morning sacrifice isn't for hours yet."

Zeus scowled.

"Who's the god here, buster?" he growled. "If I say it's sacrifice time, then it's sacrifice time, OK?"

"No," I told him. "It is quite definitely not OK. Morning sacrifice is too early as it is. If you want a sacrifice any earlier, you can do it yourself."

Zeus stuck his tongue out.

"All right then, Mister Grumpy," he said. "I jolly well will."

He opened my sock drawer and took out the old battered model temple and a bag of roast beef flavoured crisps.

I turned the light off.

In the dark, there was the rustling sound of a crisp bag being opened, and then Zeus began mumbling:

"Hmm . . . let's see. I've never really prayed to myself before. I wonder what the best way is to start? How about . . . yeah, this'll do . . . O great and mighty Me, greatest of all gods, I thank Me that I'm so great and mighty and, er, great . . . THAT'S OK, IT'S EASY REALLY. Yes, I suppose it is. Anyway, I pray that I will bring good weather today. WELL, YES, OF COURSE I WILL. ANYTHING ELSE? Yes, I pray that I will wake this stupid High Priest up so that he decides to do the sacrifice after all. YES, I CAN DO THAT, TOO. I'LL DO IT RIGHT NOW IF YOU LIKE. **WAKE UP, YOU STUPID HIGH PRIEST!**"

I sat up and turned the light on

again. Zeus was sitting with the model temple on his head and his nose in the crisp bag, but he was looking at me.

"That's better," he said. "It's no fun

praying to myself. Come on, finish the sacrifice so I can go."

"Oh, all right," I grumbled – and then I realized exactly what he'd just said. "Hang on a minute. Go? Go where?" I asked him.

"Back to Olympus, of course. I'm fed up here. It's dead boring. No one wants to die a glorious death in battle, and there aren't any roast bulls. It's more fun back home with the other gods."

"And that's it?" I demanded. "I do all this High Priesting for you, sort out all the problems you cause, sacrifice to you day and night, and you're just going to scarper?"

Zeus looked hurt.

"Of course not," he said. "You must think I've got no manners at all. No, I have a reward for my faithful High Priest."

A reward! This was more like it! Zeus was a god, after all. Maybe he was going to give me a magical wallet that never ran out of money, or a pair of football boots that always scored! Maybe even some kind of special power, like the gift of flight or the ability to talk to the animals! I looked up at him and waited.

"Yes, o loyal and trustworthy High

Priest," he told me, smiling generously, "as a reward for all your devoted service, I'm going to let you sacrifice to the other gods too!"

My face fell.

"Oh," I said sarcastically, "thanks a bunch. That's just what I wanted. Great."

"Don't mention it," Zeus smiled, missing the sarcasm completely. "But just this once, OK? Don't go sacrificing to them when I'm not around, or I might get cross."

"I don't think that'll be a problem," I said. "But I haven't got enough crisps to sacrifice to all the other gods. There are lots of them, aren't there?"

Zeus laughed. "Oh, not that sort of sacrifice," he said. "I mean the sort of sacrifice where you give up something that belongs to you."

Just for a moment, I was speechless.

"Let me get this straight," I said. "As a reward for everything I've done for you – you're going to let me give away my own property?"

Zeus grinned.

"Well," he said, "I can't go on holiday without bringing back presents for my family, can I?"

So I spent my last few hours as the High Priest of Zeus digging around in the backs of cupboards, looking for holiday souvenirs for the Greek gods of Mount Olympus. In the end, we managed to find enough for everyone,

though it wasn't easy because Zeus said each present had to have something to do with the god it was for.

Here is what Zeus finally ended up with:

* For Hera, goddess of women: one of my mum's old *Just for Women* magazines
* For Hermes, god of trickery: a joke plastic dog poo
* For Ares, god of war: a couple of toy soldiers and a water pistol
* For Aphrodite, goddess of love and beauty: a pink plastic mirror with glitter and

hearts all over it, left
by my soppy cousin
Sarah last time she
visited

★ For Hephaestus,
god of fire and
metalwork: a box of
matches and a wire
coat-hanger

★ For Artemis,
goddess of the moon:
an inflatable
spaceship

★ For Apollo, god of
music and the sun: half
a bottle of sun-screen
and a kazoo

★ For Athene,
goddess of arts and
crafts: a packet of felt-
tip pens

★ For Hades, god of the dead: this was a tricky one. Luckily while we were searching my cat came in and dropped a dead mouse at my feet. "Perfect!" Zeus said. "He'll love it!"

★ For Dionysus, god of wine and happiness: a smiley-face badge

★ For Hestia, goddess of the hearth and the hearth-fire: a lump of barbecue charcoal

★ For Demeter, goddess of the corn: a bag of tortilla chips

★ And for Poseidon, god of the sea: my old water-wings and a can of tuna

I put everything in a carrier bag and gave it to Zeus. And he disappeared.

Just like that. No "thank you", no "well done, High Priest", not even a "goodbye". He just went. And I went back to bed, feeling pretty grumpy.

I had a rotten time at school the next day. Apart from the fact that I felt so tired, I was cross with Zeus for not having said goodbye. Even though he'd been a real nuisance, I sort of missed him. The worst bit, in a way, was when Charlie – who didn't know yet that Zeus had gone – asked Miss Wise if she could read us a story about Zeus being nice to everyone and not starting any wars, and just for a moment I nodded, forgetting that Zeus wasn't there any more.

I was still in a real mood when I

got home after school. I went up to my room to get changed out of my school uniform, with something in my head still half-wondering if Zeus would be there after all. But the hamster-cage was still empty.

Or almost empty. As I glanced at it, I noticed something shiny in the corner – something that hadn't been there before.

It was a tiny golden thunderbolt on a chain. And with it was a note.